ANTHEM

THE EXCHANGE

What is the greatest threat to creativity?

ANTHEM

by

Ayn Rand

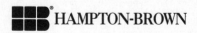 HAMPTON-BROWN

Anthem by Ayn Rand.

Cover art and design by Russ Nemec.

On-Page Coach™ (introductions, questions, on-page glossaries), The Exchange,
back cover summary, cover design © Hampton-Brown.

Hampton-Brown
P.O. Box 223220
Carmel, California 93922
800-333-3510
www.hampton-brown.com

Printed in the United States of America

ISBN-13: 978-0-7362-3159-6
ISBN-10: 0-7362-3159-5

06 07 08 09 10 11 12 13 14 15 10 9 8 7 6 5 4 3 2 1

Introduction

Ayn Rand's novel *Anthem* is set thousands of years in the future. Modern society is gone, destroyed by war long ago. The society that has been created to take its place is called the Brotherhood. In this new society, the **individual** no longer exists. People's lives do not belong to them. Instead, they exist only to work and to serve the Brotherhood. Because of this, people refer to themselves as "we." The word "I" is no longer part of the human vocabulary. People do not have names. Instead, they are numbered. Free thought and **expression** are forbidden. To be different from the group is illegal.

Rand was twelve years old when the Russian Revolution began in 1917. This was a time of great social, political, and cultural change in Russia. A new form of government

Key Concepts

individual *n.* person's own self

expression *n.* the way a person shows his or her thoughts, feelings, and beliefs called Communism eventually replaced the old political system. Communists believed in one central government that controlled the country's economy, or money. Everyone in society was treated equally. People worked together for their government or society. In exchange, the government provided the people with the things they needed to live, such as food and shelter. People did not own property or profit from their work. People were not allowed to have more or less than their neighbors.

However, Communism was not a successful form of government in Russia. Under Communism, Rand's family suffered. The Communist party took her father's business, and she and her family almost starved to death. When Rand turned twenty-one in 1926, she decided to flee to the United States to escape Communism.

The society Rand wrote about in *Anthem* was the society she thought Communism would lead to—a society where individuality is lost. Rand's novel warns readers about the dangers. *Anthem* presents a primitive world that has forgotten all its science, technology, and modern **inventions**. Rand believed that when individuality is lost, society is no longer able to **progress**. She felt that the individual creates new ideas and builds great inventions.

Key Concepts

invention *n.* an object that has never been created before

progress *v.* to advance; to develop

A society that forces the individual to **conform** makes new thought and invention impossible.

Rand believed so strongly in the importance of the individual that she created an entire philosophy that supports the idea. This philosophy is called "objectivism" and it is at the center of her novels. She believed that happiness depends on a person's ability to make choices and judgments, or their ability to reason. But only the individual mind can reason. A group cannot. In *Anthem*, Rand asks readers to consider whether or not happiness can ever exist in a world without individual thought or creativity.

The Principles of Objectivism

1. **Reality:** Individuals observe reality. They do not create the world or their own reality.

2. **Reason:** Reason is the only way for individuals to observe reality, to learn, and to survive.

3. **The Individual:** People must exist only for themselves. They must not sacrifice themselves to others or sacrifice others to themselves. Their own happiness is the reason for living.

4. **Society and Politics:** No person or group has the right to force another person to do anything. Government exists only to protect each person's individual rights.

Key Concepts

conform *v.* to change in order to be like everyone else

I

It is **a sin** to write this. It is a sin to think words no others think and to put them down upon a paper no others are to see. It is **base** and evil. It is as if we were speaking alone to no ears but our own. And we know well that there is no **transgression blacker** than to do or think alone. We have broken the laws. The laws say that men may not write unless the Council of Vocations bid them so. May we be forgiven!

But this is not the only sin upon us. We have committed a greater crime, and for this crime there is no name. What punishment awaits us if it be discovered we know not, for no such crime has come in the memory of men and there are no laws to provide for it.

It is dark here. The flame of the candle stands still in the air. Nothing moves in this tunnel **save** our hand on the paper. We are alone here under the earth. It is a fearful word, alone. The laws say that none among men may be alone, ever and at any time, for this is the great transgression and the root of all evil. But we have broken many laws. And now

....

a sin wrong, immoral
base selfish
transgression blacker crime worse
save except

there is nothing here save our one body, and it is strange to see only two legs stretched on the ground, and on the wall before us the shadow of our one head.

The walls are cracked and water runs upon them in thin threads without sound, black and glistening as blood. We stole the candle from the **larder** of the Home of the Street Sweepers. We shall be sentenced to ten years in the Palace of Corrective Detention if it be discovered. But this matters not. It matters only that the light is precious and we should not waste it to write when we need it for that work which is our crime. Nothing matters save the work, our secret, our evil, our precious work. Still, we must also write, for—may the Council have mercy on us!—we wish to speak for once to no ears but our own.

Our name is Equality 7-2521, as it is written on the iron bracelet which all men wear on their left wrists with their names upon it. We are twenty-one years old. We are six feet tall, and this is a **burden**, for there are not many men who are six feet tall. **Ever** have the Teachers and the Leaders pointed to us and frowned and said: "There is evil in your bones, Equality 7-2521, for your body has grown beyond the

....

larder pantry; supply closet
burden problem, hardship
Ever Always

bodies of your brothers." But we cannot change our bones nor our body.

We were born with a curse. It has always driven us to thoughts which are **forbidden**. It has always given us wishes which men may not wish. We know that we are evil, but there is no **will** in us and no power to resist it. This is our wonder and our secret fear, that we know and do not resist.

We strive to be like all our brother men, for all men must be alike. Over the **portals** of the Palace of the World Council, there are words cut in the marble, which we repeat to ourselves whenever we are tempted:

"We are one in all and all in one.
There are no men but only the great WE,
*One, **indivisible** and forever."*

We repeat this to ourselves, but it helps us not.

These words were cut long ago. There is green mould in the grooves of the letters and yellow streaks on the marble, which come from more years than men could count. And

....

forbidden not allowed; against the law
will ability to choose or decide
portals doors, entrance
indivisible united; unable to be divided

these words are the truth, for they are written on the Palace of the World Council, and the World Council is the **body** of all truth. Thus has it been ever since the Great Rebirth, and farther back than that no memory can reach.

But we must never speak of the times before the Great Rebirth, else we are sentenced to three years in the Palace of Corrective Detention. It is only the Old Ones who whisper about it in the evenings, in the Home of the Useless. They whisper many strange things, of the towers which rose to the sky, in those Unmentionable Times, and of the wagons which moved without horses, and of the lights which burned without flame. But those times were evil. And those times passed away, when men saw the Great Truth which is this: that all men are one and that there is no will save the will of all men together.

All men are good and wise. It is only we, Equality 7-2521, we alone who were born with a curse. For we are not like our brothers. And as we look back upon our life, we see that it has **ever been thus** and that it has brought us step by step to our last, **supreme** transgression, our crime of crimes hidden here under the ground.

....

body source
ever been thus always been this way
supreme greatest, ultimate

We remember the Home of Infants where we lived till we were five years old, together with all the children of the City who had been born in the same year. The sleeping halls there were white and clean and bare of all things save one hundred beds. We were just like all our brothers then, save for the one transgression: we fought with our brothers. There are few offenses **blacker** than to fight with our brothers, at any age and for any cause whatsoever. The Council of the Home told us so, and of all the children of that year, we were **locked in the cellar** most often.

When we were five years old, we were sent to the Home of the Students, where there are ten wards, for our ten years of learning. Men must learn till they reach their fifteenth year. Then they go to work. In the Home of the Students we arose when the big bell rang in the tower and we went to our beds when it rang again. Before we removed our garments, we stood in the great sleeping hall, and we raised our right arms, and we said all together with the three Teachers **at the head**:

"We are nothing. Mankind is all. **By the grace** of our brothers are we allowed our lives. We exist through, by and

....

blacker that are worse
locked in the cellar punished
at the head leading us
By the grace Only with the permission

for our brothers who are the State. Amen."

Then we slept. The sleeping halls were white and clean and bare of all things save one hundred beds.

We, Equality 7-2521, were not happy in those years in the Home of the Students. It was not that the learning was too hard for us. It was that the learning was too easy. This is a great sin, to be born **with a head which is too quick**. It is not good to be different from our brothers, but it is evil to be **superior to** them. The Teachers told us so, and they frowned when they looked upon us.

So we fought against this curse. We tried to forget our lessons, but we always remembered. We tried not to understand what the Teachers taught, but we always understood it before the Teachers had spoken. We looked upon Union 5-3992, who were a pale boy with only half a brain, and we tried to say and do as they did, that we might be like them, like Union 5-3992, but somehow the Teachers knew that we were not. And we were **lashed** more often than all the other children.

....

with a head which is too quick smart, intelligent
superior to better than
lashed whipped, punished

The Teachers were **just**, for they had been appointed by the Councils, and the Councils are the voice of all justice, for they are the voice of all men. And if sometimes, in the secret darkness of our heart, we regret **that which befell us** on our fifteenth birthday, we know that it was through our own guilt. We had broken a law, for we had not paid heed to the words of our Teachers. The Teachers had said to us all:

"Dare not choose in your minds the work you would like to do when you leave the Home of the Students. You shall do that which the Council of Vocations **shall prescribe for you**. For the Council of Vocations knows in its great wisdom where you are needed by your brother men, better than you can know it in your unworthy little minds. And if you are not needed by your brother men, there is no reason for you to **burden the earth with your bodies**."

We knew this well, in the years of our childhood, but our curse broke our will. We were guilty and we confess it here: we were guilty of the great Transgression of Preference. We preferred some work and some lessons to the others. We did not listen well to the history of all the Councils elected since the Great Rebirth. But we loved the

....

just fair
that which befell us what happened to us
shall prescribe for you tells you to do
burden the earth with your bodies be alive

Science of Things. We wished to know. We wished to know about all the things which make the earth around us. We asked so many questions that the Teachers **forbade it**.

We think that there are mysteries in the sky and under the water and in the plants which grow. But the Council of Scholars has said that there are no mysteries, and the Council of Scholars knows all things. And we learned much from our Teachers. We learned that the earth is flat and that the sun revolves around it, which causes the day and the night. We learned the names of all the winds which blow over the seas and push the sails of our great ships. We learned how to **bleed men** to cure them of all **ailments**.

We loved the Science of Things. And in the darkness, in the **secret hour**, when we awoke in the night and there were no brothers around us, but only their shapes in the beds and their snores, we closed our eyes, and we held our lips shut, and we stopped our breath, that no shudder might let our brothers see or hear or guess, and we thought that we wished to be sent to the Home of the Scholars when our time would come.

....

forbade it no longer allowed it
bleed men cut men and let out their blood
ailments sicknesses
secret hour middle of the night

All the great modern inventions come from the Home of the Scholars, such as the newest one, which was found only a hundred years ago, of how to make candles from wax and string; also, how to make glass, which is put in our windows to protect us from the rain. To find these things, the Scholars must study the earth and learn from the rivers, from the sands, from the winds and the rocks. And if we went to the Home of the Scholars, we could learn from these also. We could ask questions of these, for they do not forbid questions.

And questions give us no rest. We know not why our curse makes us **seek we know not what, ever and ever**. But we cannot resist it. It whispers to us that there are great things on this earth of ours, and that we can know them if we try, and that we must know them. We ask, why must we know, but it has no answer to give us. **We must know that we may know.**

So we wished to be sent to the Home of the Scholars. We wished it so much that our hands trembled under the blankets in the night, and we bit our arm to stop **that other pain which we could not endure**. It was evil and we dared

....

seek we know not what, ever and ever always ask questions

We must know that we may know. We want knowledge.

that other pain which we could not endure our mind from thinking, because we could not stand it not face our brothers in the morning. For men may wish nothing for themselves. And we were punished when the Council of Vocations came to give us our life Mandates which tell those who reach their fifteenth year what their work is to be for the rest of their days.

The Council of Vocations came on the first day of spring, and they sat in the great hall. And we who were fifteen and all the Teachers came into the great hall. And the Council of Vocations sat on a **high dais**, and they had but two words to speak to each of the Students. They called the Students' names, and when the Students stepped before them, one after another, the Council said: "Carpenter" or "Doctor" or "Cook" or "Leader." Then each Student raised their right arm and said: "The will of our brothers be done."

Now if the Council has said "Carpenter" or "Cook," the Students so assigned go to work and they do not study any further. But if the Council has said "Leader," then those Students go into the Home of the Leaders, which is the greatest house in the City, for it has three **stories**. And there they study for many years, so that they may become **candidates** and be elected to the City Council and the State

....

high dais raised platform
stories floors, levels
candidates potential leaders

20

Council and the World Council—by a free and general vote of all men. But we wished not to be a Leader, even though it is a great honor. We wished to be a Scholar.

So we awaited our turn in the great hall and then we heard the Council of Vocations call our name: "Equality 7-2521." We walked to the dais, and our legs did not tremble, and we looked up at the Council. There were five members of the Council, three of the male gender and two of the female. Their hair was white and their faces were cracked as the clay of a dry river bed. They were old. They seemed older than the marble of the Temple of the World Council. They sat before us and they did not move. And we saw no breath to stir the folds of their white **togas**. But we knew that they were alive, for a finger of the hand of the oldest rose, pointed to us, and fell down again. This was the only thing which moved, for the lips of the oldest did not move as they said: "Street Sweeper."

We felt the **cords of** our neck grow tight as our head rose higher to look upon the faces of the Council, and we were happy. We knew we had been guilty, but now we had a way to **atone for it**. We would accept our Life Mandate,

....

togas robes
cords of muscles in
atone for it fix it; make it better

and we would work for our brothers, gladly and willingly, and we would erase our sin against them, which they did not know, but we knew. So we were happy, and proud of ourselves and of our victory over ourselves. We raised our right arm and we spoke, and our voice was the clearest, the steadiest voice in the hall that day, and we said:

"The will of our brothers be done."

And we looked straight into the eyes of the Council, but their eyes were as cold blue glass buttons.

So we went into the Home of the Street Sweepers. It is a grey house on a narrow street. There is a **sundial** in its courtyard, by which the Council of the Home can tell the hours of the day and when to ring the bell. When the bell rings, we all arise from our beds. The sky is green and cold in our windows to the east. The shadow on the sundial marks off a half-hour while we dress and eat our breakfast in the dining hall, where there are five long tables with twenty clay plates and twenty clay cups on each table. Then we go to work in the streets of the City, with our brooms and our rakes. In five hours, when the sun is high, we return to

....

sundial device used to tell time

the Home and we eat our midday meal, for which one-half hour is allowed. Then we go to work again. In five hours, the shadows are blue on the pavements, and the sky is blue with a deep brightness which is not bright. We come back to have our dinner, which lasts one hour. Then the bell rings and we walk in a straight column to one of the City Halls, for the Social Meeting. Other columns of men arrive from the Homes of the different Trades. The candles are lit, and the Councils of the different Homes stand **in a pulpit**, and they speak to us of our duties and of our brother men. Then visiting Leaders mount the pulpit and they read to us the speeches which were made in the City Council that day, for the City Council represents all men and all men must know. Then we sing hymns, the Hymn of Brotherhood, and the Hymn of Equality, and the Hymn of the Collective Spirit. The sky is a soggy purple when we return to the Home. Then the bell rings and we walk in a straight column to the City Theatre for three hours of Social **Recreation**. There a play is shown upon the stage, with two great choruses from the Home of the Actors, which speak and answer all together, in two great voices. The plays are about **toil** and how good it is. Then we walk back to the Home in a straight column. The sky is like a black **sieve pierced** by silver

....

in a pulpit on a platform
Recreation Play, Entertainment
toil work
sieve pierced screen cut

drops that tremble, ready to burst through. The moths beat against the street lanterns. We go to our beds and we sleep, till the bell rings again. The sleeping halls are white and clean and bare of all things save one hundred beds.

Thus we lived each day of four years, until two springs ago when our crime happened. Thus must all men live until they are forty. At forty, they are worn out. At forty, they are sent to the Home of the Useless, where the Old Ones live. The Old Ones do not work, for the State takes care of them. They sit in the sun in summer and they sit by the fire in winter. They do not speak often, for they are **weary**. The Old Ones know that they are soon to die. When a miracle happens and some live to be forty-five, they are the Ancient Ones, and children stare at them when passing by the Home of the Useless. Such is to be our life, as that of all our brothers and of the brothers who came before us.

Such would have been our life, had we not committed our crime which changed all things for us. And it was our curse which **drove us to** our crime. We had been a good Street Sweeper and like all our brother Street Sweepers, save for our cursed wish to know. We looked too long at the

....

weary tired
drove us to made us commit

stars at night, and at the trees and the earth. And when we cleaned the yard of the Home of the Scholars, we gathered the glass **vials**, the pieces of metal, the dried bones which they had discarded. We wished to keep these things to study them, but we had no place to hide them. So we carried them to the City **Cesspool**. And then we made the discovery.

It was on a day of the spring before last. We Street Sweepers work in **brigades** of three, and we were with Union 5-3992, they of the half-brain, and with International 4-8818. Now Union 5-3992 are a sickly lad and sometimes they **are stricken with convulsions**, when their mouth froths and their eyes turn white. But International 4-8818 are different. They are a tall, strong youth and their eyes are like fireflies, for there is laughter in their eyes. We cannot look upon International 4-8818 and not smile in answer. For this they were not liked in the Home of the Students, as it is not proper to smile without reason. And also they were not liked because they took pieces of coal and they drew pictures upon the walls, and they were pictures which made men laugh. But it is only our brothers in the Home of the Artists who are permitted to draw pictures, so International 4-8818 were sent to the Home of the Street Sweepers, like ourselves.

....

vials bottles, containers
Cesspool sewer; drainage ditch
brigades groups
are stricken with convulsions have seizures

25

International 4-8818 and we are friends. This is an evil thing to say, for it is a transgression, the great Transgression of Preference, to love any among men better than the others, since we must love all men and all men are our friends. So International 4-8818 and we have never spoken of it. But we know. We know, when we look into each other's eyes. And when we look thus without words, we both know other things also, strange things for which there are no words, and these things frighten us.

So on that day **of the spring before last**, Union 5-3992 were stricken with convulsions on the edge of the City, near the City Theatre. We left them to lie in the shade of the Theatre tent and we went with International 4-8818 to finish our work. We came together to the great **ravine** behind the Theatre. It is empty save for trees and weeds. Beyond the ravine there is a **plain**, and beyond the plain there lies the **Uncharted** Forest, about which men must not think.

We were gathering the papers and the rags which the wind had blown from the Theatre, when we saw an iron bar among the weeds. It was old and rusted by many rains. We pulled with all our strength, but we could not move it. So

....

of the spring before last two years ago
ravine deep and narrow valley
plain flat piece of land
Uncharted Unexplored

we called International 4-8818, and together we **scraped** the earth around the bar. **Of a sudden** the earth fell in before us, and we saw an old iron **grill** over a black hole.

International 4-8818 stepped back. But we pulled at the grill and it gave way. And then we saw iron rings as steps leading down a shaft into a darkness without bottom.

"We shall go down," we said to International 4-8818.

"It is forbidden," they answered.

We said: "The Council does not know of this hole, so it cannot be forbidden."

And they answered: "Since the Council does not know of this hole, there can be no law permitting to enter it. And everything which is not permitted by law is forbidden."

But we said: "We shall go, **none the less**."

They were frightened, but they stood by and watched us go.

....

scraped dug
Of a sudden Immediately, Suddenly
grill covering
none the less anyway

We hung on the iron rings with our hands and our feet. We could see nothing below us. And above us the hole open upon the sky grew smaller and smaller, till it came to be the size of a button. But still we went down. Then our foot touched the ground. We rubbed our eyes, for we could not see. Then our eyes became used to the darkness, but we could not believe what we saw.

No men known to us could have built this place, nor the men known to our brothers who lived before us, and yet it was built by men. It was a great tunnel. Its walls were hard and smooth to the touch; it felt like stone, but it was not stone. On the ground there were long thin tracks of iron, but it was not iron; it felt smooth and cold as glass. We knelt, and we crawled forward, our hand **groping** along the iron line to see where it would lead. But there was an unbroken night ahead. Only the iron tracks glowed through it, straight and white, **calling us** to follow. But we could not follow, for we were losing the puddle of light behind us. So we turned and we crawled back, our hand on the iron line. And our heart beat in our fingertips, without reason. And then we knew.

We knew suddenly that this place was left from the Unmentionable Times. So it was true, and those Times had

---

groping feeling
calling us making us want

been, and all the **wonders** of those Times. Hundreds upon hundreds of years ago men knew secrets which we have lost. And we thought: "This is a **foul** place. They are **damned** who touch the things of the Unmentionable Times." But our hand which followed the track, as we crawled, clung to the iron as if it would not leave it, as if the skin of our hand were thirsty and begging of the metal some secret fluid beating in its coldness.

We returned to the earth. International 4-8818 looked upon us and stepped back.

"Equality 7-2521," they said, "your face is white."

But we could not speak and we stood looking upon them.

They backed away, as if they dared not touch us. Then they smiled, but it was not a **gay** smile; it was lost and pleading. But still we could not speak. Then they said:

"We shall report our find to the City Council and both of us will be rewarded."

And then we spoke. Our voice was hard and there was

....

wonders amazing inventions
foul bad, wicked
damned cursed
gay happy

no **mercy** in our voice. We said:

"We shall not report our find to the City Council. We shall not report it to any men."

They raised their hands to their ears, for never had they heard such words as these.

"International 4-8818," we asked, "will you report us to the Council and see us lashed to death **before your eyes**?"

They stood straight of a sudden and they answered:

"Rather would we die."

"Then," we said, "keep silent. This place is ours. This place belongs to us, Equality 7-2521, and to no other men on earth. And if ever we surrender it, we shall surrender our life with it also."

Then we saw that the eyes of International 4-8818 were full to the lids with tears they dared not drop. They whispered, and their voice trembled, so that their words **lost all shape**:

....

mercy kindness
before your eyes in front of you
lost all shape were hard to understand

"The will of the Council is above all things, for it is the will of our brothers, which is **holy**. But if you wish it so, we shall obey you. Rather shall we be evil with you than good with all our brothers. May the Council have mercy upon both our hearts!"

Then we walked away together and back to the Home of the Street Sweepers. And we walked in silence.

Thus did it **come to pass** that each night, when the stars are high and the Street Sweepers sit in the City Theatre, we, Equality 7-2521, **steal out** and run through the darkness to our place. It is easy to leave the Theatre; when the candles are blown and the Actors come onto the stage, no eyes can see us as we crawl under our seat and under the cloth of the tent. Later, it is easy to steal through the shadows and fall in line next to International 4-8818, as the column leaves the Theatre. It is dark in the streets and there are no men about, for no men may walk through the City when they have no **mission** to walk there. Each night, we run to the ravine, and we remove the stones which we have piled upon the iron grill to hide it from men. Each night, for three hours, we are under the earth, alone.

....

holy sacred; the most important thing

come to pass happen

steal out leave, escape

mission reason, purpose

We have stolen candles from the Home of the Street Sweepers, we have stolen **flints** and knives and paper, and we have brought them to this place. We have stolen glass vials and powders and acids from the Home of the Scholars. Now we sit in the tunnel for three hours each night and we study. We melt strange metals, and we mix acids, and we cut open the bodies of the animals which we find in the City Cesspool. We have built an oven of the bricks we gathered in the streets. We burn the wood we find in the ravine. The fire flickers in the oven and blue shadows dance upon the walls, and there is no sound of men to disturb us.

We have stolen **manuscripts**. This is a great **offense**. Manuscripts are precious, for our brothers in the Home of the Clerks spend one year to copy one single script in their clear handwriting. Manuscripts are rare and they are kept in the Home of the Scholars. So we sit under the earth and we read the stolen scripts. Two years have passed since we found this place. And in these two years we have learned more than we had learned in the ten years of the Home of the Students.

....

flints stones for making fire
manuscripts documents
offense crime

We have learned things which are not in the scripts. We have solved secrets of which the Scholars have no knowledge. We have come to see how great is the unexplored, and many lifetimes will not bring us to the end of our **quest**. But we wish no end to our quest. We wish nothing, save to be alone and to learn, and to feel as if with each day our sight were growing sharper than the hawk's and clearer than rock crystal.

Strange are the ways of evil. We are false in the faces of our brothers. We are defying the will of our Councils. We alone, of the thousands who walk this earth, we alone in this hour are doing a work which has no purpose save that we wish to do it. The evil of our crime is not for the human mind to probe. The nature of our punishment, if it be discovered, is not for the human heart to **ponder**. Never, not in the memory of the Ancient Ones' Ancients, never have men done that which we are doing.

And yet there is no shame in us and no regret. We say to ourselves that we are **a wretch and a traitor**. But we feel no burden upon our spirit and no fear in our heart. And it

....

quest search, investigation

probe explore, examine

ponder know; think about

a wretch and a traitor a terrible person

seems to us that our spirit is clear as a lake troubled by no eyes save those of the sun. And in our heart—strange are the ways of evil!—in our heart there is the first peace we have known in twenty years.

BEFORE YOU MOVE ON...

1. **Narrator** The narrator, E-72521, tells the story using "we" instead of "I." Why does he tell it this way?

2. **Setting** Reread pages 18–19. The story takes place in the future. What else can you tell about the setting?

LOOK AHEAD Read pages 35–50 to find out who Equality 7-2521 meets and how this affects him.

II

Liberty 5-3000 . . . Liberty five-three thousand . . . Liberty 5-3000 . . .

We wish to write this name. We wish to speak it, but we dare not speak it above a whisper. For men are forbidden to take notice of women, and women are forbidden to take notice of men. But we think of one among women, they whose name is Liberty 5-3000, and we think of no others.

The women who have been assigned to work the soil live in the Homes of the Peasants beyond the City. Where the City ends there is a great road winding off to the north, and we Street Sweepers must keep this road clean **to the first milepost**. There is a hedge along the road, and beyond the hedge lie the fields. The fields are black and **ploughed**, and they lie like a great fan before us, with their furrows gathered in some hand beyond the sky, spreading forth from that hand, opening wide apart as they come toward us, like black pleats that sparkle with thin, green spangles. Women work in the fields, and their white tunics

....

to the first milepost for one mile from the city
ploughed prepared for planting

in the wind are like the wings of sea-gulls beating over the black soil.

And there it was that we saw Liberty 5-3000 walking along the furrows. Their body was straight and thin as a blade of iron. Their eyes were dark and hard and glowing, with no fear in them, no kindness and no guilt. Their hair was golden as the sun; their hair flew in the wind, shining and wild, as if it **defied** men to restrain it. They threw seeds from their hand **as if they deigned to fling a scornful gift, and the earth was a beggar under their feet**.

We stood still; for the first time did we know fear, and then pain. And we stood still that we might not **spill** this pain more precious than pleasure.

Then we heard a voice from the others call their name: "Liberty 5-3000," and they turned and walked back. Thus we learned their name, and we stood watching them go, till their white tunic was lost in the blue mist.

And the following day, as we came to the northern road, we kept our eyes upon Liberty 5-3000 in the field. And each

....

defied dared

as if they deigned to fling a scornful gift, and the earth was a beggar under their feet carelessly

spill lose

day thereafter we knew the illness of waiting for our hour on the northern road. And there we looked at Liberty 5-3000 each day. We know not whether they looked at us also, but we think they did.

Then one day they came close to the hedge, and suddenly they turned to us. They **turned in a whirl** and the movement of their body stopped, as if **slashed** off, as suddenly as it had started. They stood still as a stone, and they looked straight upon us, straight into our eyes. There was no smile on their face, and no welcome. But their face was **taut**, and their eyes were dark. Then they turned as swiftly, and they walked away from us.

But the following day, when we came to the road, they smiled. They smiled to us and for us. And we smiled in answer. Their head fell back, and their arms fell, as if their arms and their thin white neck were stricken suddenly with a great **lassitude**. They were not long looking upon us, but upon the sky. Then they glanced at us over their shoulder, and we felt as if a hand had touched our body, slipping softly from our lips to our feet.

....

turned in a whirl spun around quickly
slashed cut
taut tense
lassitude tiredness

Every morning thereafter, we greeted each other with our eyes. We dared not speak. It is a transgression to speak to men of other Trades, save in groups at the Social Meetings. But once, standing at the hedge, we raised our hand to our forehead and then moved it slowly, palm down, toward Liberty 5-3000. Had the others seen it, they could have guessed nothing, for it looked only as if we were **shading** our eyes from the sun. But Liberty 5-3000 saw it and understood. They raised their hand to their forehead and moved it as we had. Thus, each day, we greet Liberty 5-3000, and they answer, and no men **can suspect**.

We do not wonder at this new sin of ours. It is our second Transgression of Preference, for we do not think of all our brothers, as we must, but only of one, and their name is Liberty 5-3000. We do not know why we think of them. We do not know why, when we think of them, we feel of a sudden that the earth is good and that it is **not a burden to live**.

We do not think of them as Liberty 5-3000 any longer. We have given them a name in our thoughts. We call them the Golden One. But it is a sin to give men names which

....

shading protecting, covering
can suspect understand what we are doing
not a burden to live good to be alive

distinguish them from other men. Yet we call them the Golden One, for they are not like the others. The Golden One are not like the others.

And we **take no heed of** the law which says that men may not think of women, save at the Time of Mating. This is the time each spring when all the men older than twenty and all the women older than eighteen are sent for one night to the City Palace of Mating. And each of the men have one of the women assigned to them by the Council of **Eugenics**. Children are born each winter, but women never see their children and children never know their parents. Twice have we been sent to the Palace of Mating, but it is an ugly and **shameful matter**, of which we do not like to think.

We had broken so many laws, and today we have broken one more. Today, we spoke to the Golden One.

The other women were far off in the field, when we stopped at the hedge by the side of the road. The Golden One were kneeling alone at the **moat** which runs through the field. And the drops of water falling from their hands, as they raised the water to their lips, were like sparks of

....

take no heed of do not obey
Eugenics Controlled Breeding
shameful matter embarrassing experience
moat ditch filled with water

fire in the sun. Then the Golden One saw us, and they did not move, kneeling there, looking at us, and circles of light **played** upon their white tunic, from the sun on the water of the moat, and one sparkling drop fell from a finger of their hand held as frozen in the air.

Then the Golden One rose and walked to the hedge, as if they had heard a command in our eyes. The two other Street Sweepers of our brigade were a hundred **paces** away down the road. And we thought that International 4-8818 would not betray us, and Union 5-3992 would not understand. So we looked straight upon the Golden One, and we saw the shadows of their lashes on their white cheeks and the sparks of sun on their lips. And we said:

"You are beautiful, Liberty 5-3000."

Their face did not move and they did not **avert their eyes**. Only their eyes grew wider, and there was **triumph** in their eyes, and it was not triumph over us, but over things we could not guess. Then they asked:

"What is your name?"

....

played shone
paces steps
avert their eyes look away
triumph victory, joy

"Equality 7-2521," we answered.

"You are not one of our brothers, Equality 7-2521, for we do not wish you to be."

We cannot say what they meant, for there are no words for their meaning, but we know it without words and we knew it then.

"No," we answered, "nor are you one of our sisters."

"If you see us among **scores of** women, will you look **upon us**?"

"We shall look upon you, Liberty 5-3000, if we see you among all the women of the earth."

Then they asked:

"Are Street Sweepers sent to different parts of the City or do they always work in the same places?"
"They always work in the same places," we answered, "and no one will take this road away from us."

....

scores of many; large numbers of
upon us at us

"Your eyes," they said, "are not like the eyes of any **among men**."

And suddenly, without **cause for the thought which came to us**, we felt cold, cold to our stomach.

"How old are you?" we asked.

They understood our thought, for they lowered their eyes for the first time.

"Seventeen," they whispered.

And we sighed, as if a burden had been taken from us, for we had been thinking without reason of the Palace of Mating. And we thought that we would not let the Golden One be sent to the Palace. How to prevent it, how to **bar** the will of the Councils, we knew not, but we knew suddenly that we would. Only we do not know why such thought came to us, for these ugly matters bear no relation to us and the Golden One. What relation can they bear?

Still, without reason, as we stood there by the hedge, we

....

among men others
cause for the thought which came to us knowing why
bar stop, halt

felt our lips drawn tight with hatred, a sudden hatred for all our brother men. And the Golden One saw it and smiled slowly, and there was in their smile the first sadness we had seen in them. We think that in the wisdom of women the Golden One had understood more than we can understand.

Then three of the sisters in the field appeared, coming toward the road, so the Golden One walked away from us. They took the bag of seeds, and they threw the seeds into the **furrows** of earth as they walked away. But the seeds **flew wildly**, for the hand of the Golden One was trembling.

Yet as we walked back to the Home of the Street Sweepers, we felt that we wanted to sing, without reason. So we were **reprimanded** tonight, in the dining hall, for without knowing it we had begun to sing aloud some tune we had never heard. But it is not proper to sing without reason, save at the Social Meetings.

"We are singing because we are happy," we answered the one of the Home Council who reprimanded us.

"Indeed you are happy," they answered. "How else can

---

furrows rows
flew wildly did not land in the rows
reprimanded scolded; spoken to angrily

men be when they live for their brothers?"

And now, sitting here in our tunnel, we wonder about these words. It is forbidden, not to be happy. For, as it has been explained to us, men are free and the earth belongs to them; and all things on earth belong to all men; and the will of all men together is good for all; and so all men must be happy.

Yet as we stand at night in the great hall, removing our garments for sleep, we look upon our brothers and we wonder. The heads of our brothers are bowed. The eyes of our brothers are **dull**, and never do they look one another in the eyes. The shoulders of our brothers are hunched, and their muscles are drawn, as if their bodies were shrinking and wished to **shrink out of sight**. And a word **steals** into our mind, as we look upon our brothers, and that word is fear.

There is fear hanging in the air of the sleeping halls, and in the air of the streets. Fear walks through the City, fear **without name, without shape**. All men feel it and none dare to speak.

....

dull not bright or happy-looking
shrink out of sight become so small they disappear
steals comes
without name, without shape of the unknown

We feel it also, when we are in the Home of the Street Sweepers. But here, in our tunnel, we feel it no longer. The air is pure under the ground. There is no odor of men. And these three hours give us strength for our hours above the ground.

Our body is betraying us, for the Council of the Home looks with suspicion upon us. It is not good to feel too much joy nor to be glad that our body lives. For we matter not and it must not matter to us whether we live or die, which is to be as our brothers will it. But we, Equality 7-2521, are glad to be living. **If this is a vice, then we wish no virtue.**

Yet our brothers are not like us. All is not well with our brothers. There are Fraternity 2-5503, a quiet boy with wise, kind eyes, who cry suddenly, without reason, in the **midst** of day or night, and their body shakes with sobs they cannot explain. There are Solidarity 9-6347, who are a bright youth, without fear in the day; but they scream in their sleep, and they scream: "Help us! Help us! Help us!" into the night, in a voice which chills our bones, but the Doctors cannot cure Solidarity 9-6347.

....

If this is a vice, then we wish no virtue. If this is wrong, then we do not want to be right.

midst middle

And as we all undress at night, in the dim light of the candles, our brothers are silent, for they dare not speak the thoughts of their minds. For all must agree with all, and they cannot know if their thoughts are the thoughts of all, and so they fear to speak. And they are glad when the candles are blown for the night. But we, Equality 7-2521, look through the window upon the sky, and there is peace in the sky, and cleanliness, and dignity. And beyond the City there lies the plain, and beyond the plain, black upon the black sky, there lies the Uncharted Forest.

We do not wish to look upon the Uncharted Forest. We do not wish to think of it. But **ever do** our eyes return to that black patch upon the sky. Men never enter the Uncharted Forest, for there is no **power** to explore it and no path to lead among its ancient trees which stand as guards of fearful secrets. It is whispered that once or twice in a hundred years, one among the men of the City escape alone and run to the Uncharted Forest, without **call** or reason. These men do not return. They **perish** from hunger and from the claws of the wild beasts which roam the Forest. But our Councils say that this is only a legend. We have heard that there are many Uncharted Forests over the land,

....

ever do often, frequently

power way

call sense

perish die

46

among the Cities. And it is whispered that they have grown over the **ruins** of many cities of the Unmentionable Times. The trees have swallowed the ruins, and the bones under the ruins, and all the things which perished.

And as we look upon the Uncharted Forest far in the night, we think of the secrets of the Unmentionable Times. And we wonder how it came to pass that these secrets were lost to the world. We have heard the legends of the great fighting, in which many men fought on one side and only a few on the other. These few were the Evil Ones and they were **conquered**. Then great fires raged over the land. And in these fires the Evil Ones and all the things made by the Evil Ones were burned. And the fire which is called the Dawn of the Great Rebirth, was the Script Fire where all the scripts of the Evil Ones were burned, and with them all the words of the Evil Ones. Great mountains of flame stood in the **squares** of the Cities for three months. Then came the Great Rebirth.

The words of the Evil Ones . . . The words of the Unmentionable Times . . . What are the words which we have lost?

....

ruins remains
conquered beaten, defeated
squares centers

May the Council have mercy upon us! We had no wish to write such a question, and we knew not what we were doing till we had written it. We shall not ask this question and we shall not think it. We shall not **call death upon our head**.

And yet . . . And yet . . .

There is some word, one single word which is not in the language of men, but which had been. And this is the Unspeakable Word, which no men may speak nor hear. But sometimes, and it is rare, sometimes, somewhere, one among men find that word. They find it upon scraps of old manuscripts or cut into the fragments of ancient stones. But when they speak it they are **put to death**. There is no crime punished by death in this world, save this one crime of speaking the Unspeakable Word.

We have seen one of such men burned alive in the square of the City. And it was a sight which has stayed with us through the years, and it haunts us, and follows us, and it gives us no rest. We were a child then, ten years old. And we stood in the great square with all the children and all the

....

call death upon our head write things which will get us killed
if they are discovered
put to death killed

men of the City, sent to **behold** the burning. They brought the Transgressor out into the square and they led them to the **pyre**. They had torn out the tongue of the Transgressor, so that they could speak no longer. The Transgressor were young and tall. They had hair of gold and eyes of blue as morning. They walked to the pyre, and their step did not **falter**. And of all the faces on that square, of all the faces which shrieked and screamed and spat curses upon them, theirs was the calmest and the happiest face.

As the chains were wound over their body at the stake, and a flame set to the pyre, the Transgressor looked upon the City. There was a thin thread of blood running from the corner of their mouth, but their lips were smiling. And a monstrous thought came to us then, which has never left us. We had heard of Saints. There are the Saints of Labor, and the Saints of the Councils, and the Saints of the Great Rebirth. But we had never seen a Saint nor what the likeness of a Saint should be. And we thought then, standing in the square, that the likeness of a Saint was the face we saw before us in the flames, the face of the Transgressor of the Unspeakable Word.

....

behold watch
pyre pile of wood where they would be burned
falter hesitate

As the flames rose, a thing happened which no eyes saw but ours, else we would not be living today. Perhaps it had only seemed to us. But it seemed to us that the eyes of the Transgressor had chosen us from the crowd and were looking straight upon us. There was no pain in their eyes and no knowledge of the **agony** of their body. There was only joy in them, and pride, a pride holier than it is fit for human pride to be. And it seemed as if these eyes were trying to tell us something through the flames, to send into our eyes some word without sound. And it seemed as if these eyes were begging us to gather that word and not to let it go from us and from the earth. But the flames rose and we could not guess the word . . .

What—even if we have to burn for it like the Saint of the pyre—what is the Unspeakable Word?

....

agony pain

BEFORE YOU MOVE ON...

1. **Character** On pages 40–42, why does Equality 7-2521 speak to Liberty 5-3000? What does this tell you about him?

2. **Inference** Reread page 47. Who were the Evil Ones? Why were they evil?

LOOK AHEAD Go on to pages 51–68 to find out the amazing discovery Equality 7-2521 makes in the tunnel.

III

We, Equality 7-2521, have discovered a new power of nature. And we have discovered it alone, and we are alone to know it.

It is said. Now let us be lashed for it, if we must. The Council of Scholars has said that we all know the things which exist and therefore the things which are not known by all do not exist. But we think that the Council of Scholars is **blind**. The secrets of this earth are not for all men to see, but only for those who will **seek** them. We know, for we have found a secret unknown to all our brothers.

We know not what this power is nor **whence** it comes. But we know its nature, we have watched it and worked with it. We saw it first two years ago. One night, we were cutting open the body of a dead frog when we saw its leg jerking. It was dead, yet it moved. Some power unknown to men was making it move. We could not understand it. Then, after many tests, we found the answer. The frog had

....

blind not looking for these things
seek try to find; search for
whence from where

been hanging on a wire of copper; and it had been the metal of our knife which had sent a strange power to the copper through the **brine of** the frog's body. We put a piece of copper and a piece of zinc into a jar of brine, we touched a wire to them, and there, under our fingers, was a miracle which had never occurred before, a new miracle and a new power.

This discovery haunted us. We **followed it in preference to** all our studies. We worked with it, we tested it in more ways than we can describe, and each step was as another miracle **unveiling** before us. We came to know that we had found the greatest power on earth. For it defies all the laws known to men. It makes the needle move and turn on the compass which we stole from the Home of the Scholars; but we had been taught, when still a child, that the **loadstone** points to the north and that this is a law which nothing can change; yet our new power defies all laws. We found that it causes lightning, and never have men known what causes lightning. In thunderstorms, we raised a tall rod of iron by the side of our hole, and we watched it from below. We have seen the lightning strike it again and again. And now we know that metal draws the power of the

....

brine of liquids in
followed it in preference to felt it it was more important than
unveiling revealed
loadstone magnet

sky, and that metal can be made to give it forth.

We have built strange things with this discovery of ours. We used for it the copper wires which we found here under the ground. We have walked the length of our tunnel, with a candle lighting the way. We could go no farther than half a mile, for earth and rock had fallen at both ends. But we gathered all the things we found and we brought them to our work place. We found strange boxes with bars of metal inside, with many cords and **strands** and coils of metal. We found wires that led to strange little globes of glass on the walls; they contained threads of metal thinner than a spider's web.

These things help us in our work. We do not understand them, but we think that the men of the Unmentionable Times had known our power of the sky, and these things had some **relation** to it. We do not know, but we shall learn. We cannot stop now, even though it frightens us that we are alone in our knowledge.

No single one can possess greater wisdom than the many Scholars who are elected by all men for their wisdom.

....

strands wires
relation connection

Yet we can. We do. We have fought against saying it, but now it is said. We do not care. We forget all men, all laws and all things save our metals and our wires. So much is still to be learned! **So long a road lies before us, and what care we if we must travel it alone!**

···

So long a road lies before us, and what care we if we must travel it alone! There is so much to learn and we do not care if we are the only one who learns it!

IV

Many days passed before we could speak to the Golden One again. But then came the day when the sky turned white, as if the sun had burst and spread its flame in the air, and the fields lay still without **breath**, and the dust of the road was white in the glow. So the women of the field were weary, and they **tarried over** their work, and they were far from the road when we came. But the Golden One stood alone at the hedge, waiting. We stopped and we saw that their eyes, so **hard and scornful** to the world, were looking at us as if they would obey any word we might speak. And we said:

"We have given you a name in our thoughts, Liberty 5-3000."

"What is our name?" they asked.

"The Golden One."

"Nor do we call you Equality 7-2521 when we think of you."

....

breath wind
tarried over very slowly did
hard and scornful cold and angry

"What name have you given us?"

They looked straight into our eyes and they held their head **high** and they answered:

"The Unconquered."

For a long time we could not speak. Then we said:

"Such thoughts as these are forbidden, Golden One."

"But you think such thoughts as these and you wish us to think them."

We looked into their eyes and we could not lie.

"Yes," we whispered, and they smiled, and then we said: "Our dearest one, do not obey us."

They stepped back, and their eyes were wide and **still**.

"Speak these words again," they whispered.

....

high proudly
still stared at us

"Which words?" we asked. But they did not answer, and we knew it.

"Our dearest one," we whispered.

Never have men said this to women.

The head of the Golden One bowed slowly, and they stood still before us, their arms at their sides, the palms of their hands turned to us, as if **their body were delivered in submission to our eyes**. And we could not speak.

Then they raised their head, and they spoke simply and gently, as if they wished us to forget some **anxiety** of their own.

"The day is hot," they said, "and you have worked for many hours and you must be weary."

"No," we answered.

"It is cooler in the fields," they said, "and there is water to drink. Are you thirsty?"

....

their body were delivered in submission to our eyes they stood there just so we could look at them

anxiety worry

"Yes," we answered, "but we cannot cross the hedge."

"We shall bring the water to you," they said.

Then they knelt by the moat, they gathered water in their two hands, they rose and they held the water out to our lips.

We do not know if we drank that water. We only knew suddenly that their hands were empty, but we were still holding our lips to their hands, and that they knew it, but did not move.

We raised our head and stepped back. For we did not understand what had made us do this, and we were afraid to understand it.

And the Golden One stepped back, and stood looking upon their hands in **wonder**. Then the Golden One moved away, even though no others were coming, and they moved **stepping back,** as if they could not turn from us, their arms bent before them, as if they could not lower their hands.

....

wonder amazement
stepping back backwards

V

We made it. We created it. We brought it forth from the night of the ages. We alone. Our hands. Our mind. Ours alone and only.

We know not what we are saying. Our head is **reeling**. We look upon the light which we have made. We shall be forgiven for anything we say tonight. . . .

Tonight, after more days and **trials** than we can count, we finished building a strange thing, from the remains of the Unmentionable Times, a box of glass, devised to give forth the power of the sky of greater strength than we had ever achieved before. And when we put our wires to this box, when we **closed the current**—the wire glowed! It came to life, it turned red, and a circle of light lay on the stone before us.

We stood, and we held our head in our hands. We could not **conceive of** that which we had created. We had touched no flint, made no fire. Yet here was light, light that came

....

reeling dizzy
trials attempts
closed the current connected the wires
conceive of believe

from nowhere, light from the heart of metal.

We blew out the candle. Darkness swallowed us. There was nothing left around us, nothing save night and a thin thread of flame in it, as a crack in the wall of a prison. We stretched our hands to the wire, and we saw our fingers in the red glow. We could not see our body nor feel it, and in that moment nothing existed save our two hands over a wire glowing in a black **abyss**.

Then we thought of the meaning of that which lay before us. We can light our tunnel, and the City, and all the Cities of the world with nothing save metal and wires. We can give our brothers a new light, cleaner and brighter than any they have ever known. The power of the sky can be made to do **men's bidding**. There are no limits to its secrets and its **might**, and it can be made to **grant us** anything if we but choose to ask.

Then we knew what we must do. Our discovery is too great for us to waste our time in sweeping the streets. We must not keep our secret to ourselves, nor buried under the ground. We must bring it into the sight of all men. We need

....

abyss hole
men's bidding what we want it to do
might strength, power
grant us do

all our time, we need the work rooms of the Home of the Scholars, we want the help of our brother Scholars and their wisdom joined to ours. There is so much work ahead for all of us, for all the Scholars of the world.

In a month, the World Council of Scholars is to meet in our City. It is a great Council, to which the wisest of all lands are elected, and it meets once a year in the different Cities of the earth. We shall go to this Council and we shall lay before them, as our gift, the glass box with the power of the sky. We shall **confess everything to them**. They will see, understand and forgive. **For our gift is greater than our transgression.** They will explain it to the Council of Vocations, and we shall be assigned to the Home of the Scholars. This has never been done before, but neither has a gift such as ours ever been offered to men.

We must wait. We must guard our tunnel as we had never guarded it before. For should any men save the Scholars learn of our secret, they would not understand it, nor would they believe us. They would see nothing, save our crime of working alone, and they would destroy us and our light. We care not about our body, but our light is . . .

....

confess everything to them tell them everything we have done

For our gift is greater than our transgression. This discovery is more important than our crime.

Yes, we do care. For the first time do we care about our body. For this wire is a part of our body, as a vein torn from us, glowing with our blood. Are we proud of this thread of metal, or of our hands which made it, or is there a line to divide these two?

We stretch out our arms. For the first time do we know how strong our arms are. And a strange thought comes to us: we wonder, for the first time in our life, what we look like. Men never see their own faces and never ask their brothers about it, for it is evil to **have concern for** their own faces or bodies. But tonight, for a reason we cannot **fathom**, we wish it were possible to us to know **the likeness of our own person**.

....

have concern for care about
fathom understand
the likeness of our own person what we look like

VI

We have not written for thirty days. For thirty days we have not been here, in our tunnel. We had been caught.

It happened on that night when we wrote last. We forgot, that night, to watch the **sand in the glass** which tells us when three hours have passed and it is time to return to the City Theatre. When we remembered it, the sand had run out.

We **hastened** to the Theatre. But the big tent stood grey and silent against the sky. The streets of the City lay before us, dark and empty. If we went back to hide in our tunnel, we would be found and our light found with us. So we walked to the Home of the Street Sweepers.

When the Council of the Home questioned us, we looked upon the faces of the Council, but there was no curiosity in those faces, and no anger, and no mercy. So when the oldest of them asked us: "Where have you been?" we thought of our glass box and of our light, and we forgot

....

sand in the glass hourglass
hastened ran, rushed

all else. And we answered:

"We will not tell you."

The oldest did not question us **further**. They turned to the two youngest, and said, and their voice was bored:

"Take our brother Equality 7-2521 to the Palace of Corrective Detention. Lash them until they tell."

So we were taken to the Stone Room under the Palace of Corrective Detention. This room has no windows and it is empty save for an iron post. Two men stood by the post, naked but for leather aprons and leather hoods over their faces. Those who had brought us **departed**, leaving us to the two Judges who stood in a corner of the room. The Judges were small, thin men, grey and bent. They gave the signal to the two strong hooded ones.

They tore our clothes from our body, they threw us down upon our knees and they tied our hands to the iron post.

The first blow of the lash felt as if our spine had been

....

further again
departed left

cut in two. The second blow **stopped the first**, and for a second we felt nothing, then the pain struck us in our throat and fire ran in our lungs without air. But we did not cry out.

The lash whistled like a singing wind. We tried to count the blows, but we lost count. We knew that the blows were falling upon our back. Only we felt nothing upon our back any longer. A flaming grill kept dancing before our eyes, and we thought of nothing save that grill, a grill, a grill of red squares, and then we knew that we were looking at the squares of the iron grill in the door, and there were also the squares of stone on the walls, and the squares which the lash was cutting upon our back, crossing and re-crossing itself in our flesh.

Then we saw a fist before us. It knocked our chin up, and we saw the red **froth** of our mouth on the **withered** fingers, and the Judge asked:

"Where have you been?"

But we jerked our head away, hid our face upon our tied hands, and bit our lips.

....

stopped the first made us forget the pain of the first blow
froth blood and spit
withered old and wrinkled

The lash whistled again. We wondered who was sprinkling burning coal dust upon the floor, for we saw drops of red twinkling on the stones around us.

Then we knew nothing, save two voices **snarling steadily**, one after the other, even though we knew they were speaking many minutes apart:

"Where have you been where have you been where have you been where have you been? . . ."

And our lips moved, but the sound trickled back into our throat, and the sound was only:

"The light . . . The light . . . The light. . . ."

Then we knew nothing.

We opened our eyes, lying on our stomach on the brick floor of a **cell**. We looked upon two hands lying far before us on the bricks, and we moved them, and we knew that they were our hands. But we could not move our body. Then we smiled, for we thought of the light and that we had

....

snarling steadily repeating angrily
cell prison

not **betrayed it**.

We lay in our cell for many days. The door opened twice each day, once for the men who brought us bread and water, and once for the Judges. Many Judges came to our cell, first the **humblest** and then the most honored Judges of the City. They stood before us in their white togas, and they asked:

"Are you ready to speak?"

But we shook our head, lying before them on the floor. And they departed.

We counted each day and each night as it passed. Then, tonight, we knew that we must escape. For tomorrow the World Council of Scholars is to meet in our City.

It was easy to escape from the Palace of Corrective Detention. The locks are old on the doors and there are no guards about. There is no reason to have guards, for men have never defied the Councils so far as to escape from whatever place they were ordered to be. Our body is healthy

....

betrayed it told anyone about it
humblest lowest

and strength returns to it speedily. We lunged against the door and it **gave way**. We **stole** through the dark passages, and through the dark streets, and down into our tunnel.

We lit the candle and we saw that our place had not been found and nothing had been touched. And our glass box stood before us on the cold oven, as we had left it. What matter they now, the scars upon our back!

Tomorrow, in the full light of day, we shall take our box, and leave our tunnel open, and walk through the streets to the Home of the Scholars. We shall put before them the greatest gift ever offered to men. We shall tell them the truth. We shall hand to them, as our confession, these pages we have written. We shall join our hands to theirs, and we shall work together, with the power of the sky, for the glory of mankind. Our blessing upon you, our brothers! Tomorrow, you will take us back into your **fold** and we shall be an **outcast** no longer. Tomorrow we shall be one of you again. Tomorrow . . .

....

gave way opened
stole moved carefully
fold city
outcast outsider

BEFORE YOU MOVE ON...

1. **Character's Motive** Why will Equality 7-2521 tell only the Scholars about his discovery?

2. **Cause and Effect** Equality 7-2521 is jailed for being late. Why does he escape?

LOOK AHEAD What happens at the Home of the Scholars? Read pages 69–92 to find out.

VII

It is dark here in the forest. The leaves **rustle** over our head, black against the last gold of the sky. The **moss** is soft and warm. We shall sleep on this moss for many nights, till the **beasts** of the forest come to tear our body. We have no bed now, save the moss, and no future, save the beasts.

We are old now, yet we were young this morning, when we carried our glass box through the streets of the City to the Home of the Scholars. No men stopped us, for there were none about from the Palace of Corrective Detention, and the others knew nothing. No men stopped us at the gate. We walked through empty passages and into the great hall where the World Council of Scholars sat in **solemn** meeting.

We saw nothing as we entered, save the sky in the great windows, blue and glowing. Then we saw the Scholars who sat around a long table; they were as shapeless clouds huddled at the rise of the great sky. There were men whose famous names we knew, and others from distant lands

....

rustle move in the wind
moss ground
beasts animals
solemn serious

69

whose names we had not heard. We saw a great painting on the wall over their heads, of the twenty **illustrious** men who had invented the candle.

All the heads of the Council turned to us as we entered. These great and wise of the earth did not know what to think of us, and they looked upon us with wonder and curiosity, as if we were a miracle. It is true that our tunic was torn and stained with brown stains which had been blood. We raised our right arm and we said:

"Our greeting to you, our **honored** brothers of the World Council of Scholars!"

Then Collective 0-0009, the oldest and wisest of the Council, spoke and asked:

"Who are you, our brother? For you do not look like a Scholar."

"Our name is Equality 7-2521," we answered, "and we are a Street Sweeper of this City."

---

illustrious famous and important
honored respected

Then it was as if a great wind had **stricken** the hall, for all the Scholars spoke at once, and they were angry and frightened.

"A Street Sweeper! A Street Sweeper walking in upon the World Council of Scholars! It is not to be believed! It is against all the rules and all the laws!"

But we knew how to stop them.

"Our brothers!" we said. "We matter not, nor our transgression. It is only our brother men who matter. Give no thought to us, for we are nothing, but listen to our words, for we bring you a gift such as has never been brought to men. Listen to us, for we hold the future of mankind in our hands."

Then they listened.

We placed our glass box upon the table before them. We spoke of it, and of our long quest, and of our tunnel, and of our escape from the Palace of Corrective Detention. Not a hand moved in that hall, as we spoke, nor an eye. Then we

----

stricken blown through

put the wires to the box, and they all bent forward and sat still, watching. And we stood still, our eyes upon the wire. And slowly, slowly as a flush of blood, a red flame trembled in the wire. Then the wire glowed.

But terror struck the men of the Council. They leapt to their feet, they ran from the table, and they stood pressed against the wall, huddled together, seeking the warmth of one another's bodies to give them courage.

We looked upon them and we laughed and said:

"Fear nothing, our brothers. There is a great power in these wires, but this power is **tamed**. It is yours. We give it to you."

Still they would not move.

"We give you the power of the sky!" we cried. "We give you the key to the earth! Take it, and let us be one of you, the humblest among you. Let us all work together, and **harness** this power, and make it **ease the toil** of men. Let us throw away our candles and our torches. Let us flood our

....

tamed controlled
harness learn to control
ease the toil help the work

cities with light. Let us bring a new light to men!"

But they looked upon us, and suddenly we were afraid.
For their eyes were still, and small, and evil.

"Our brothers!" we cried. "Have you nothing to say
to us?"

Then Collective 0-0009 moved forward. They moved to
the table and the others followed.

"Yes," spoke Collective 0-0009, "we have much to say
to you."

The sound of their voice brought silence to the hall and
to the beat of our heart.

"Yes," said Collective 0-0009, "we have much to say to
a wretch who have broken all the laws and who **boast of
their infamy**! How dared you think that your mind held
greater wisdom than the minds of your brothers? And if the
Councils had **decreed** that you should be a Street Sweeper,
how dared you think that you could be of greater use to men

....

boast of their infamy brag about their crimes
decreed decided

73

than in sweeping the streets?"

"How dared you, gutter cleaner," spoke Fraternity 9-3452, "to hold yourself as one alone and with the thoughts of the one and not of the many?"

"You shall be burned at the stake," said Democracy 4-6998.

"No, they shall be lashed," said Unanimity 7-3304, "till there is nothing left under the lashes."

"No," said Collective 0-0009, "we cannot decide upon this, our brothers. No such crime has ever been committed, and it is not for us to judge. Nor for any small Council. We shall deliver this creature to the World Council itself and **let their will be done**."

We looked upon them and we **pleaded**:

"Our brothers! You are right. Let the will of the Council be done upon our body. We do not care. But the light? What will you do with the light?"

....

let their will be done let them decide what to do
pleaded begged

Collective 0-0009 looked upon us, and they smiled.

"So you think that you have found a new power," said Collective 0-0009. "Do all your brothers think that?"

"No," we answered.

"What is not thought by all men cannot be true," said Collective 0-0009.

"You have worked on this alone?" asked International 1-5537.

"Yes," we answered.

"What is not done **collectively** cannot be good," said International 1-5537.

"Many men in the Homes of the Scholars have had strange new ideas in the past," said Solidarity 8-1164, "but when the majority of their brother Scholars voted against them, they abandoned their ideas, as all men must."

---

collectively together; as a group

"This box is useless," said Alliance 6-7349.

"Should it be **what they claim of it**," said Harmony 9-2642, "then it would bring ruin to the Department of Candles. The Candle is a great **boon** to mankind, as approved by all men. Therefore it cannot be destroyed by the **whim** of one."

"This would wreck the Plans of the World Council," said Unanimity 2-9913, "and without the Plans of the World Council the sun cannot rise. It took fifty years to secure the approval of all the Councils for the Candle, and to decide upon the number needed, and to re-fit the Plans so as to make candles instead of torches. This **touched upon** thousands and thousands of men working in scores of States. We cannot alter the Plans again so soon."

"And if this should lighten the toil of men," said Similarity 5-0306, "then it is a great evil, for men have no cause to exist save in toiling for other men."

Then Collective 0-0009 rose and pointed at our box.

"This thing," they said, "must be destroyed."

....

what they claim of it   as great as they say it is
boon   help, benefit
whim   sudden idea
touched upon   affected

And all the others cried as one:

"It must be destroyed!"

Then we leapt to the table.

We seized our box, we shoved them aside, and we ran to the window. We turned and we looked at them for the last time, and a rage, such as it is not fit for humans to know, choked our voice in our throat.

"You fools!" we cried. "You fools! You thrice-damned fools!"

We swung our fist through the windowpane, and we leapt out in a ringing rain of glass.

We fell, but we never let the box fall from our hands. Then we ran. We ran **blindly**, and men and houses streaked past us in a **torrent** without shape. And the road seemed not to be flat before us, but as if it were leaping up to meet us, and we waited **for the earth to rise and strike us in the face**. But we ran. We knew not where we were going. We

....

blindly not knowing where to go

torrent blur

for the earth to rise and strike us in the face to trip and œfall down knew only that we must run, run to the end of the world, to the end of our days.

Then we knew suddenly that we were lying on a soft earth and that we had stopped. Trees taller than we had ever seen before stood over us in a great silence. Then we knew. We were in the Uncharted Forest. We had not thought of coming here, but our legs had carried our wisdom, and our legs had brought us to the Uncharted Forest **against our will**.

Our glass box lay beside us. We crawled to it, we fell upon it, our face in our arms, and we lay still.

We lay thus for a long time. Then we rose, we took our box, and walked on into the forest.

It mattered not where we went. We knew that men would not follow us, for they never enter the Uncharted Forest. We had nothing to fear from them. **The forest disposes of its own victims.** This gave us no fear either. Only we wished to be away, away from the City and from the air that touches upon the air of the City. So we walked

....

against our will without our knowledge

The forest disposes of its own victims. People disappear in the forest.

on, our box in our arms, our heart empty.

We are doomed. Whatever days are left to us, we shall spend them alone. And we have heard of the **corruption** to be found in solitude. We have torn ourselves from the truth which is our brother men, and there is no road back for us, and no **redemption**.

We know these things, but we do not care. We care for nothing on earth. We are tired.

Only the glass box in our arms is like a living heart that gives us strength. We have lied to ourselves. We have not built this box for the good of our brothers. We built it **for its own sake**. It is above all our brothers to us, and its truth above their truth. Why wonder about this? We have not many days to live. We are walking to **the fangs** awaiting us somewhere among the great, silent trees. There is not a thing behind us to regret.

Then a blow of pain struck us, our first and our only. We thought of the Golden One. We thought of the Golden One whom we shall never see again. Then the pain passed.

....

corruption danger
redemption way to rejoin our brothers
for its own sake in order to learn
the fangs death

79

It is best. We are one of the Damned. It is best if the Golden One forget our name and the body **which bore** that name.

....

which bore who was called

VIII

It has been a day of wonder, this, our first day in the forest.

We awoke when a ray of sunlight fell across our face. We wanted to leap to our feet, as we have had to leap every morning of our life, but we remembered suddenly that no bell had rung and that there was no bell to ring anywhere. We lay on our back, we threw our arms out, and we looked up at the sky. The leaves had edges of silver that trembled and rippled like a river of green and fire flowing high above us.

We did not wish to move. We thought suddenly that we could lie thus as long as we wished, and we laughed aloud at the thought. We could also rise, or run, or leap, or fall down again. We were thinking that these were thoughts without sense, but before we knew it our body had risen in one leap. Our arms stretched out of their own will, and our body **whirled and whirled**, till it raised a wind to rustle through the leaves of the bushes. Then our hands seized a branch and swung us high into a tree, with no **aim** save the

....

whirled and whirled spun around in a circle
aim purpose

wonder of learning the strength of our body. The branch snapped under us and we fell upon the moss that was soft as a cushion. Then our body, losing all sense, rolled over and over on the moss, dry leaves in our tunic, in our hair, in our face. And we heard suddenly that we were laughing, laughing aloud, laughing as if there were no power left in us save laughter.

Then we took our glass box, and we went on into the forest. We went on, cutting through the branches, and it was as if we were swimming through a sea of leaves, with the bushes as waves rising and falling and rising around us, and flinging their green **sprays** high to the treetops. The trees parted before us, calling us forward. The forest seemed to welcome us. We went on, without thought, without care, with nothing to feel save the song of our body.

We stopped when we felt hunger. We saw birds in the tree branches, and flying from under our footsteps. We picked a stone and we **sent it as an arrow** at a bird. It fell before us. We made a fire, we cooked the bird, and we ate it, and no meal had ever tasted better to us. And we thought suddenly that there was a great satisfaction to be found in

....

sprays branches
sent it as an arrow threw it

the food which we need and **obtain by our own hand**. And we wished to be hungry again and soon, that we might know again this strange new pride in eating.

Then we walked on. And we came to a stream which lay as a streak of glass among the trees. It lay so still that we saw no water but only a cut in the earth, in which the trees grew down, upturned, and the sky lay at the bottom. We knelt by the stream and we bent down to drink. And then we stopped. For, upon the **blue of the sky below us**, we saw our own face for the first time.

We sat still and we held our breath. For our face and our body were beautiful. Our face was not like the faces of our brothers, for we felt no **pity** when looking upon it. Our body was not like the bodies of our brothers, for our limbs were straight and thin and hard and strong. And we thought that we could trust this being who looked upon us from the stream, and that we had nothing to fear with this being.

We walked on till the sun had set. When the shadows gathered among the trees, we stopped in a hollow between the roots, where we shall sleep tonight. And suddenly, for

....

obtain by our own hand get for ourselves
blue of the sky below us reflection of the sky in the water
pity sadness

the first time this day, we remembered that we are the Damned. We remembered it, and we laughed.

We are writing this on the paper we had hidden in our tunic together with the written pages we had brought for the World Council of Scholars, but never given to them. We have much to speak of to ourselves, and we hope we shall find the words for it in the **days to come**. Now, we cannot speak, for we cannot understand.

....

days to come future

IX

We have not written for many days. We did not wish to speak. For we needed no words to remember that which has happened to us.

It was on our second day in the forest that we heard steps behind us. We hid in the bushes, and we waited. The steps came closer. And then we saw the fold of a white tunic among the trees, and a gleam of gold.

We leapt forward, we ran to them, and we stood looking upon the Golden One.

They saw us, and their hands closed into fists, and the fists pulled their arms down, as if they wished their arms to hold them, while their body **swayed**. And they could not speak.

We dared not come too close to them. We asked, and our voice trembled:

....

swayed moved from side to side

"How come you to be here, Golden One?"

But they whispered only:

"We have found you. . . ."

"How come you to be in the forest?" we asked.

They raised their head, and there was a great pride in their voice; they answered:

"We have followed you."

Then we could not speak, and they said:

"We heard that you had gone to the Uncharted Forest, for the whole City is speaking of it. So on the night of the day when we heard it, we ran away from the Home of the Peasants. We found **the marks of your feet** across the plain where no men walk. So we followed them, and we went into the forest, and we followed the path where the branches were broken by your body."

....

the marks of your feet your footprints

Their white tunic was torn, and the branches had cut the skin of their arms, but they spoke as if they had never **taken notice of** it, nor of weariness, nor of fear.

"We have followed you," they said, "and we shall follow you wherever you go. If danger threatens you, we shall face it also. If it be death, we shall die with you. You are damned, and we wish to share your damnation."

They looked upon us, and their voice was low, but there was bitterness and triumph in their voice:

"Your eyes are **as a flame**, but our brothers have neither hope nor fire. Your mouth is **cut of granite**, but our brothers are soft and humble. Your head is high, but our brothers **cringe**. You walk, but our brothers crawl. We wish to be damned with you, rather than blessed with all our brothers. Do as you please with us, but do not send us away from you."

Then they knelt, and bowed their golden head before us.

We had never thought of that which we did. We bent

....

taken notice of noticed, felt
as a flame bright, alive
cut of granite firm and strong
cringe bow their heads

to raise the Golden One to their feet, but when we touched them, it was as if **madness had stricken us**. We seized their body and we pressed our lips to theirs. The Golden One breathed once, and their breath was a moan, and then their arms closed around us.

We stood together for a long time. And we were frightened that we had lived for twenty-one years and had never known what joy is possible to men.

Then we said:

"Our dearest one. Fear nothing of the forest. There is no danger in solitude. We have no need of our brothers. Let us forget their good and our evil, let us forget all things save that we are together and that there is joy **as a bond between us**. Give us your hand. Look ahead. It is our own world, Golden One, a strange, unknown world, but our own."

Then we walked on into the forest, their hand in ours.

And that night we knew that to hold the body of women

....

madness had stricken us we had become crazy
as a bond between us in being together

in our arms is neither ugly nor shameful, but the one **ecstasy granted** to the race of men.

We have walked for many days. The forest has no end, and we seek no end. But each day added to the chain of days between us and the City is like an added blessing.

We have made a bow and many arrows. We can kill more birds than we need for our food; we find water and fruit in the forest. At night, we choose a clearing, and we build a ring of fires around it. We sleep in the midst of that ring, and the beasts dare not attack us. We can see their eyes, green and yellow as coals, watching us from the tree branches beyond. The fires **smolder** as a crown of jewels around us, and smoke stands still in the air, in columns made blue by the moonlight. We sleep together in the midst of the ring, the arms of the Golden One around us, their head upon our breast.

Some day, we shall stop and build a house, when we shall have gone far enough. But we do not have to **hasten**. The days before us are without end, like the forest.

....

ecstasy granted joy given
smolder burn
hasten hurry

We cannot understand this new life which we have found, yet it seems so clear and so simple. When questions come to puzzle us, we walk faster, then turn and forget all things as we watch the Golden One following. The shadows of leaves fall upon their arms, as they spread the branches apart, but their shoulders are in the sun. The skin of their arms is like a blue mist, but their shoulders are white and glowing, as if the light fell not from above, but rose from under their skin. We watch the leaf which has fallen upon their shoulder, and it lies at the curve of their neck, and a drop of **dew glistens** upon it like a jewel. They approach us, and they stop, laughing, knowing what we think, and they wait obediently, without questions, till it pleases us to turn and go on.

We go on and we bless the earth under our feet. But questions come to us again, as we walk in silence. If that which we have found is the corruption of solitude, then what can men wish for save corruption? If this is the great evil of being alone, then what is good and what is evil?

Everything which comes from the many is good. Everything which comes from one is evil. Thus have we

....

dew glistens rain shines

been taught **with our first breath**. We have broken the law, but we have never **doubted it**. Yet now, as we walk through the forest, we are learning to doubt.

There is no life for men, save in useful toil for the good of all their brothers. But we lived not, when we toiled for our brothers, we were only weary. There is no joy for men, save the joy shared with all their brothers. But the only things which taught us joy were the power we created in our wires, and the Golden One. And both these joys belong to us alone, they come from us alone, they **bear no relation** to our brothers, and they do not concern our brothers in any way. Thus do we wonder.

There is some error, one frightful error, in the thinking of men. What is that error? We do not know, but the knowledge struggles within us, struggles to be born.

Today, the Golden One stopped suddenly and said:

"We love you."

But then they frowned and shook their head and looked

....

with our first breath since birth
doubted it thought the law was wrong
bear no relation have no connection

at us helplessly.

"No," they whispered, "that is not what we wished to say."

They were silent, then they spoke slowly, and their words were **halting**, like the words of a child learning to speak for the first time:

"We are one . . . alone . . . and only . . . and we love you who are one . . . alone . . . and only."

We looked into each other's eyes and we knew that the breath of a miracle had touched us, and fled, and left us **groping vainly**.

And we felt **torn, torn for** some word we could not find.

....

halting hesitant

groping vainly searching unsuccessfully

torn, torn for frustrated and helpless because of

BEFORE YOU MOVE ON...

1. **Summarize** Reread pages 70–77. How do the Scholars react to Equality 7-2521 and his discovery?

2. **Plot** Reread pages 81–84. How does Equality 7-2521's life change after he runs from the Scholars?

LOOK AHEAD Read pages 93–113 to find out how Equality 7-2521 plans to change the world.

X

We are sitting at a table and we are writing this upon paper
made thousands of years ago. The light is **dim**, and we
cannot see the Golden One, only one lock of gold on the
pillow of an ancient bed. This is our home.

We came upon it today, at sunrise. For many days we
had been crossing a chain of mountains. The forest rose
among cliffs, and whenever we walked out upon **a barren**
stretch of rock we saw great peaks before us in the west, and
to the north of us, and to the south, as far as our eyes could
see. The peaks were red and brown, with the green streaks
of forests as veins upon them, with blue mists as veils over
their heads. We had never heard of these mountains, nor
seen them marked on any map. The Uncharted Forest
has protected them from the Cities and from the men
of the Cities.

We climbed paths where the wild goat dared not follow.
Stones rolled from under our feet, and we heard them
striking the rocks below, farther and farther down, and the

....

dim low
a barren an empty

mountains **rang** with each stroke, and long after the strokes had died. But we went on, for we knew that no men would ever follow our track nor reach us here.

Then today, at sunrise, we saw a white flame among the trees, high on a **sheer** peak before us. We thought that it was a fire and we stopped. But the flame was unmoving, yet blinding as liquid metal. So we climbed toward it through the rocks. And there, before us, on a **broad summit**, with the mountains rising behind it, stood a house such as we had never seen, and the white fire came from the sun on the glass of its windows.

The house had two stories and a strange roof flat as a floor. There was more window than wall upon its walls, and the windows went on straight around the corners, though how this kept the house standing we could not guess. The walls were hard and smooth, of that stone unlike stone which we had seen in our tunnel.

We both knew it without words: this house was left from the Unmentionable Times. The trees had protected it from time and weather, and from men who have less pity than

....

rang echoed
sheer tall, steep
broad summit wide mountain peak

time and weather. We turned to the Golden One and
we asked:

"Are you afraid?"

But they shook their head. So we walked to the door,
and we threw it open, and we stepped together into the
house of the Unmentionable Times.

We shall need the days and the years ahead, to look,
to learn and to understand the things of this house. Today,
we could only look and try to believe the sight of our eyes.
We pulled the heavy curtains from the windows and we
saw that the rooms were small, and we thought that not
more than twelve men could have lived here. We thought
it strange that men had been permitted to build a house for
only twelve.

Never had we seen rooms so full of light. **The sunrays
danced upon colors**, colors, more colors than we thought
possible, we who had seen no houses save the white ones,
the brown ones and the grey. There were great pieces of
glass on the walls, but it was not glass, for when we looked

....

The sunrays danced upon colors The sunlight showed colors
everywhere

upon it we saw our own bodies and all the things behind us, as on the **face** of a lake. There were strange things which we had never seen and the use of which we do not know. And there were globes of glass everywhere, in each room, the globes with the metal cobwebs inside, such as we had seen in our tunnel.

We found the sleeping hall and we stood in **awe upon its threshold**. For it was a small room and there were only two beds in it. We found no other beds in the house, and then we knew that only two had lived here, and this **passes understanding**. What kind of world did they have, the men of the Unmentionable Times?

We found garments, and the Golden One gasped at the sight of them. For they were not white tunics, nor white togas; they were of all colors, no two of them alike. Some crumbled to dust as we touched them. But others were of heavier cloth, and they felt soft and new in our fingers.

We found a room with walls made of shelves, which held rows of manuscripts, from the floor to the ceiling. Never had we seen such a number of them, nor of such strange

---

face surface

awe upon its threshold amazement in the doorway

passes understanding did not make sense to us

shape. They were not soft and rolled, they had hard shells of cloth and leather; and the letters on their pages were so small and so even that we wondered at the men who had such handwriting. We glanced through the pages, and we saw that they were written in our language, but we found many words which we could not understand. Tomorrow, we shall begin to read these scripts.

When we had seen all the rooms of the house, we looked at the Golden One and we both knew the thought in our minds.

"We shall never leave this house," we said, "nor let it be taken from us. This is our home and the end of our journey. This is your house, Golden One, and ours, and it belongs to no other men **whatever as far as the earth may stretch**. We shall not share it with others, as we share not our joy with them, nor our love, nor our hunger. So be it **to the end of our days**."

"Your will be done," they said.

Then we went out to gather wood for the great **hearth**

....

whatever as far as the earth may stretch in the world
to the end of our days until we die
hearth fireplace

of our home. We brought water from the stream which runs among the trees under our windows. We killed a mountain goat, and we brought its flesh to be cooked in a strange copper pot we found in a place of wonders, which must have been the cooking room of the house.

We did this work alone, for no words of ours could take the Golden One away from the big glass which is not glass. They stood before it and they looked and looked upon their own body.

When the sun sank beyond the mountains, the Golden One fell asleep on the floor, **amidst** jewels, and bottles of crystal, and flowers of silk. We lifted the Golden One in our arms and we carried them to a bed, their head falling softly upon our shoulder. Then we lit a candle, and we brought paper from the room of the manuscripts, and we sat by the window, for we knew that we could not sleep tonight.

And now we look upon the earth and sky. This **spread** of naked rock and peaks and moonlight is like a world ready to be born, a world that waits. It seems to us it asks a sign from us, a spark, a first commandment. We cannot know

....

amidst in the middle of
spread view

what word we are to give, nor what great deed this earth expects to **witness**. We know it waits. It seems to say it has great gifts to lay before us, but it wishes a greater gift from us. We are to speak. We are to give its goal, its highest meaning to all this glowing space of rock and sky.

We look ahead, we beg our heart for **guidance** in answering this call no voice has spoken, yet we have heard. We look upon our hands. We see the dust of centuries, the dust which hid great secrets and perhaps great evils. And yet it stirs no fear within our heart, but only silent **reverence and pity**.

May knowledge come to us! What is the secret our heart has understood and yet will not reveal to us, although it seems to beat as if it were **endeavoring** to tell it?

....

witness see
guidance help, direction
reverence and pity respect and sadness
endeavoring trying

XI

I am. I think. I will.

My hands . . . My spirit . . . My sky . . . My forest . . .
This earth of mine . . .

What must I say besides? These are the words. This is
the answer.

I stand here on the **summit** of the mountain. I lift
my head and I spread my arms. This, my body and spirit,
this is the end of the quest. I wished to know the meaning
of things. I am the meaning. I wished to find a **warrant
for being**. I need no warrant for being, and **no word
of sanction upon my being**. I am the warrant and the
sanction.

It is my eyes which see, and the sight of my eyes grants
beauty to the earth. It is my ears which hear, and the
hearing of my ears gives its song to the world. It is my
mind which thinks, and the judgment of my mind is the

....

summit top

warrant for being reason for living

no word of sanction upon my being no need to ask
permission to live

only searchlight that can find the truth. It is my will which chooses, and the choice of my will is the only **edict** I must respect.

Many words have been granted me, and some are wise, and some are false, but only three are holy: "I will it!"

Whatever road I take, the guiding star is within me; the guiding star and the loadstone which point the way. They point in but one direction. They point to me.

I know not if this earth on which I stand is the **core** of the universe or if it is but a speck of dust lost in eternity. I know not and I care not. For I know what happiness is possible to me on earth. And my happiness **needs no higher aim to vindicate it**. My happiness is not the **means to any end**. It is the end. It is its own goal. It is its own purpose.

Neither am I the means to any end others may wish to accomplish. I am not a tool for their use. I am not a servant of their needs. I am not a bandage for their wounds. I am not a sacrifice on their altars.

....

edict law
core center
needs no higher aim to vindicate it does not need a purpose
means to any end way to get something else

I am a man. This miracle of me is mine to own and keep, and mine to guard, and mine to use, and mine to kneel before!

I do not surrender my treasures, nor do I share them. The fortune of my spirit is not to be blown into coins of brass and flung to the winds as **alms** for the poor of the spirit. I guard my treasures: my thought, my will, my freedom. And the greatest of these is freedom.

I owe nothing to my brothers, nor do **I gather debts from them**. I ask none to live for me, nor do I live for any others. I **covet** no man's soul, nor is my soul theirs to covet.

I am neither foe nor friend to my brothers, but such as each of them shall deserve of me. And to earn my love, my brothers must do more than to have been born. I do not grant my love without reason, nor to any **chance passer-by** who may wish to claim it. I honor men with my love. But honor is a thing to be earned.

I shall choose friends among men, but neither slaves nor masters. And I shall choose only such as please me, and

....

alms charity
I gather debts from them they owe me anything
covet want, desire
chance passer-by people around me

them I shall love and respect, but neither command nor obey. And we shall join our hands when we wish, or walk alone when we so desire. For in the temple of his spirit, each man is alone. Let each man keep his **temple untouched and undefiled**. Then let him join hands with others if he wishes, but only beyond his holy threshold.

For the word "We" must never be spoken, save by one's choice and as a second thought. This word must never be placed first within man's soul, else it becomes a monster, the root of all the evils on earth, the root of man's torture by men, and of an unspeakable lie.

The word "We" is as lime poured over men, which sets and hardens to stone, and crushes all beneath it, and **that which is white and that which is black are lost equally in the grey of it**. It is the word by which the depraved steal the virtue of the good, by which the weak steal the might of the strong, by which the fools steal the wisdom of the sages.

What is my joy if all hands, even the unclean, can reach into it? What is my wisdom, if even the fools can dictate to me? What is my freedom, if all creatures, even the

....

temple untouched and undefiled spirit whole and pure

that which is white and that which is black are lost equally in the grey of it the difference between good and evil becomes unclear

botched and impotent, are my masters? What is my life, if I am but to bow, to agree and to obey?

But I am done with this **creed** of corruption.

I am done with the monster of "We," the word of **serfdom**, of **plunder**, of misery, falsehood and shame.

And now I see the face of god, and I raise this god over the earth, this god whom men have sought since men came into being, this god who will grant them joy and peace and pride.

This god, this one word:

"I."

....

botched and impotent flawed, weak
creed system, philosophy
serfdom slavery
plunder force

XII

It was when I read the first of the books I found in my house that I saw the word "I." And when I understood this word, the book fell from my hands, and I wept, I who had never known tears. I wept in **deliverance** and in pity for all mankind.

I understood the blessed thing which I had called my curse. I understood why the best in me had been my sins and my transgressions; and why I had never felt guilt in my sins. I understood that centuries of chains and lashes will not kill the **spirit** of man nor the sense of truth within him.

I read many books for many days. Then I called the Golden One, and I told her what I had read and what I had learned. She looked at me and the first words she spoke were:

"I love you."

Then I said:

....
deliverance freedom
spirit strength

"My dearest one, it is not proper for men to be without names. There was a time when each man had a name of his own to distinguish him from all other men. So let us choose our names. I have read of a man who lived many thousands of years ago, and of all the names in these books, his is the one I wish to **bear**. He took the light of the gods and he brought it to men, and he taught men to be gods. And he suffered for his deed as all bearers of light must suffer. His name was Prometheus."

"It shall be your name," said the Golden One.

"And I have read of a goddess," I said, "who was the mother of the earth and of all the gods. Her name was Gaea. Let this be your name, my Golden One, for you are to be the mother of a new kind of gods."

"It shall be my name," said the Golden One.

Now I look ahead. My future is clear before me. The **Saint of the pyre** had seen the future when he chose me as **his heir**, as the heir of all the saints and all the **martyrs** who came before him and who died for the same cause,

....

bear have, use
Saint of the pyre man I saw burned alive
his heir the one to follow him
martyrs people who died for their beliefs

106

for the same word, no matter what name they gave to their cause and their truth.

I shall live here, in my own house. I shall take my food from the earth by the toil of my own hands. I shall learn many secrets from my books. Through the years ahead, I shall rebuild the achievements of the past, and open the way to carry them further, the achievements which are open to me, but closed forever to my brothers, for their minds are **shackled** to the weakest and dullest ones among them.

I have learned that my power of the sky was known to men long ago; they called it Electricity. It was the power that moved their greatest inventions. It lit this house with light which came from those globes of glass on the walls. I have found the engine which produced this light. I shall learn how to repair it and how to make it work again. I shall learn how to use the wires which carry this power. Then I shall build a barrier of wires around my home, and across the paths which lead to my home; a barrier light as a cobweb, more **impassable** than a wall of granite; a barrier my brothers will never be able to cross. For they have nothing to fight me with, save the **brute force** of their

....

shackled tied, bound, chained
impassable of a barrier
brute force strength

numbers. I have my mind.

Then here, on this mountaintop, with the world below me and nothing above me but the sun, I shall live my own truth. Gaea is pregnant with my child. Our son will be raised as a man. He will be taught to say "I" and to **bear the pride** of it. He will be taught to walk straight and on his own feet. He will be taught **reverence** for his own spirit.

When I shall have read all the books and learned my new way, when my home will be ready and my earth tilled, I shall **steal** one day, for the last time, into the cursed City of my birth. I shall call to me my friend who has no name save International 4-8818, and all those like him, Fraternity 2-5503, who cries without reason, and Solidarity 9-6347 who calls for help in the night, and a few others. I shall call to me all the men and the women whose spirit has not been killed within them and who suffer under the **yoke** of their brothers. They will follow me and I shall lead them to my fortress. And here, in this uncharted wilderness, I and they, my chosen friends, my fellow-builders, shall write the first chapter in the new history of man.

....

bear the pride be proud
reverence respect
steal go, sneak
yoke imprisonment, enslavement

These are the things before me. And as I stand here at the door of glory, I look behind me for the last time. I look upon the history of men, which I have learned from the books, and I wonder. It was a long story, and the spirit which moved it was the spirit of man's freedom. But what is freedom? Freedom from what? There is nothing to take a man's freedom away from him, save other men. To be free, a man must be free of his brothers. That is freedom. That and nothing else.

At first, man was enslaved by the gods. But he broke their chains. Then he was enslaved by the kings. But he broke their chains. He was enslaved by his birth, by his **kin**, by his race. But he broke their chains. He declared to all his brothers that a man has rights which neither god nor king nor other men can take away from him, no matter what their number, for his is the right of man, and there is no right on earth **above** this right. And he stood on the threshold of the freedom for which the blood of the centuries behind him had been spilled.

But then he gave up all he had won, and fell lower than his **savage** beginning.

....

kin family
above more important than
savage wild, rough

What **brought it to pass**? What disaster took their reason away from men? What whip lashed them to their knees in shame and **submission**? The worship of the word "We."

When men accepted that worship, the structure of centuries collapsed about them, the structure whose every beam had come from the thought of some one man, each in his day down the ages, from the depth of some one spirit, such spirit as existed but for its own sake. Those men who survived—those eager to obey, eager to live for one another, since they had nothing else to **vindicate them**—those men could neither carry on, nor preserve what they had received. Thus did all thought, all science, all wisdom perish on earth. Thus did men—men with nothing to offer save their great numbers—lose the steel towers, the flying ships, the power wires, all the things they had not created and could never keep. Perhaps, later, some men had been born with the mind and the courage to recover these things which were lost; perhaps these men came before the Councils of Scholars. They were answered as I have been answered— and for the same reasons.

....

brought it to pass caused this to happen
submission defeat
vindicate them justify their existence

But I still wonder how it was possible, in those graceless years of transition, long ago, that men did not see **whither** they were going, and went on, in blindness and **cowardice**, to their fate. I wonder, for it is hard for me to conceive how men who knew the word "I," could give it up and not know what they lost. But such has been the story, for I have lived in the City of the damned, and I know what horror men permitted to be brought upon them.

Perhaps, in those days, there were a few among men, a few of clear sight and clean soul, who refused to surrender that word. What agony must have been theirs before that which they saw coming and could not stop! Perhaps they cried out in protest and in warning. But men **paid no heed** to their warning. And they, these few, fought a hopeless battle, and they perished with their banners smeared by their own blood. And they chose to perish, for they knew. To them, I send my **salute** across the centuries, and my pity.

Theirs is the banner in my hand. And I wish I had the power to tell them that the despair of their hearts was not to be final, and their night was not without hope. For the battle they lost can never be lost. For that which they died

....

whither the direction
cowardice fear
paid no heed did not listen
salute regards

to save can never perish. Through all the darkness, through all the shame of which men are capable, the spirit of man will remain alive on this earth. It may sleep, but it will awaken. It may wear chains, but it will break through. And man will go on. Man, not men.

Here, on this mountain, I and my sons and my chosen friends shall build our new land and our **fort**. And it will become as the heart of the earth, lost and hidden at first, but beating, beating louder each day. And word of it will reach every corner of the earth. And the roads of the world will become as veins which will carry the best of the world's blood to my threshold. And all my brothers, and the Councils of my brothers, will hear of it, but they will be **impotent** against me. And the day will come when I shall break all the chains of the earth, and **raze** the cities of the enslaved, and my home will become the capital of a world where each man will be free to exist for his own sake.

For the coming of that day shall I fight, I and my sons and my chosen friends. For the freedom of Man. For his rights. For his life. For his honor.

....

fort society
impotent powerless
raze destroy

And here, over the portals of my fort, I shall cut in the stone the word which is to be my **beacon and my banner**. The word which will not die, should we all perish in battle. The word which can never die on this earth, for it is the **heart** of it and the meaning and the **glory**.

The sacred word:

EGO

....

beacon and my banner guide and my motto
heart center, core
glory beauty
EGO INDIVIDUALITY; THE SELF

BEFORE YOU MOVE ON...

1. **Character's Motive** Reread page 108. Why does Equality 7-2521 plan to someday return to the city?

2. **Paraphrase** What does Equality 7-2521 mean when he says, "To be free, a man must be free of his brothers"?